Ben's Biscuit Tin Adventure

First Edition

To Emilia
and
Gwen

Loos of Love,

xx.

Published by the Nazca Plains Corporation

Las Vegas, Nevada

2015

ISBN: 978-1-61098-214-6
E-Book: 978-1-61098-215-3

Published by:

The Nazca Plains Corporation®
Austin TX 78755

PUBLISHER'S NOTE

Illustrated by Ryan Doherty
Art Director, Kimm Antell

To Ben Elliott and his brother Daniel,
whose skill at acquiring extra biscuits
at bedtime inspired this story.

Jenny
X

To Ted,
who I'm sure will be getting his
hands on the biscuit tin in no
time.

Ryan
X

Ben's Biscuit Tin Adventure

First Edition

Written by Jenny Kane
Illustrated by Ryan Doherty

The biscuit tin is kept in the kitchen, at the back of the **highest** shelf in the **tallest** cupboard.

It's a square tin, cream on the outside and blue on the inside. On the front, the word **BISCUITS** is written in **big** black letters.

Usually there are plain biscuits in the tin. Sometimes there are even ginger nuts or custard creams.

Now and again, if I'm *really* good,
Mum buys cookies or even
chocolate biscuits. **YUMMY!!!!!**

I *love* biscuits, but Dad says too
many are bad for me. Dad says
that's why they're hidden away at the
back of the **highest** shelf of the
tallest cupboard.

Mum says they are hidden away at the back of the **highest** shelf of the **tallest** cupboard because Dad *loves* biscuits even more than I do...

and if the tin was handy, he'd eat them **all** himself!

Every evening, before my brother Dan and I clean our teeth, Mum gives each of us **two** biscuits and a glass of milk.

Last night, even after my biscuit supper, I was still hungry. My tummy *rumbled* and *grumbled* as I snuggled into bed, and I began to wonder how I could get another biscuit.

I'm only seven and I'm only short!

Lying in bed, I began to hatch a plan...

I'll wait until Mum and Dad are
asleep, then I'll creep
quietly
down
the stairs...

and taking care not to let the door squeak, I'll sneak into the kitchen, open a drawer, and take out some string and some **double-sided sticky tape.**

Then, I'll stand on a chair and open
the cupboard door.

Taking the string, I'll make a cowboy lasso. Then, I'll stick **loads** of double-sided tape to the end of the lasso, and toss it up to the shelf, where it will fall around the biscuit tin.

I'll gently pull the lasso, so that the biscuit tin comes closer and **closer** and **closer**...
Now comes the tricky bit...

Just as I get the tin to the edge of the shelf, I'll stand underneath it, and with a massive *heave* on the string, the tin would fall into my hands. No, that wouldn't work, the tin might fly off, and...

CRASH!!!!

There would be smashed biscuits
everywhere. Mum and Dad would
wake up and I'd be in **BIG** trouble.

I need a new plan.

I'll wait until Mum and Dad are
asleep, then I'll creep
quietly
down
the stairs...

and taking care not to let the door squeak, I'll sneak into the kitchen and arrange my building blocks **up** and **up** and **UP** beneath the cupboard.

I'd build my blue, red, and yellow bricks **higher** and **higher** until they're tall enough for me to stand on and reach the biscuit tin.

But the blocks might not be strong enough! They could collapse under my weight and...

CRASH!!!!!

Mum and Dad would wake up and I'd
be in **BIG** trouble.

I need a new plan.

I'll wait until Mum and Dad are
asleep. Then, I'll creep
quietly
down
the stairs...

and taking care not to let the door squeak, I'll jump onto a pair of stilts. Balancing carefully, I'll stand by the **highest** shelf of the **tallest** cupboard, and grab the biscuit tin.

But what if, just as I got ready to seize the tin, I slipped off my stilts and...

CRASH!!!!!

Mum and Dad would wake up and I'd be in **BIG** trouble.

I need a new plan.

I'll wait until Mum and Dad are asleep,
then, I'll creep
quietly
down
the stairs...

and taking care not to let the door squeak, I'll sneak into the kitchen and find some *springy* springs. Then, I'll tie them to my feet...

bounce up to the cupboard, and grab the tin!

I think that might work.

It would work.

I'm *sure* it would work...
HOORAY!!!

I jumped up to celebrate and woke myself up. **OH NO!!** It was only a dream!!! I was still thinking about my biscuit tin adventure when I heard Mum shouting, "Ben, Ben!!"

Climbing out of bed, I headed downstairs in my pyjamas. When I got to the kitchen, I couldn't believe my eyes... there was string, sticky tape, building blocks, stilts, springs, a chair...

and

biscuit crumbs all over the floor!!!

"Ben?" asked Mum, shaking her head as she looked at the mess, "Why didn't you just ask me for another biscuit?"

Maybe it wasn't a dream after all.

The End.

Jenny Kane is the author of quirky children's picture books *There's a Cow in the Flat* (Hush Puppy, 2014) and *Ben's Biscuit Tin Adventure* (Hush Puppy, 2015). Jenny also writes contemporary romance novels, including *Abi's House* (Accent Press, 2015), *Romancing Robin Hood* (Accent Press, 2014), and the bestselling novel *Another Cup of Coffee* (Accent Press, 2013). Jenny's fourth full length novel, *Another Glass of Champagne,* will be published by Accent Press in 2016. Keep your eye on Jenny's blog at www.jennykane.co.uk for more details.
Twitter- @JennyKaneAuthor
Facebook- https://www.facebook.com/JennyKaneRomance

Ryan Doherty is the illustrator of the children's books *There's a Cow in the Flat* (Hush Puppy, 2014) and *Ben's Biscuit Tin Adventure* (Hush Puppy, 2015). He studied illustration at the University of Central Lancashire and is currently living in the Northwest of England. To receive news on upcoming work by Ryan Doherty, you can follow him on Twitter at @artofryan1 or you can email him at ryandohertyillustrations@gmail.com.

Made in the USA
Charleston, SC
17 August 2015